NARROWBOAT GODDESS

A SAILING ROMANCE STORY

M. L. BUCHMAN

PRAISE FOR M. L. BUCHMAN

A fabulous soaring thriller.

— *TAKE OVER AT MIDNIGHT*, MIDWEST
BOOK REVIEW

Meticulously researched, hard-hitting, and suspenseful.

— *PURE HEAT*, PUBLISHERS WEEKLY,
STARRED REVIEW

Expert technical details abound, as do realistic military missions with superb imagery that will have readers feeling as if they are right there in the midst and on the edges of their seats.

— *LIGHT UP THE NIGHT*, RT REVIEWS, 4
1/2 STARS

Buchman has catapulted his way to the top tier of my favorite authors.

— FRESH FICTION

Nonstop action that will keep readers on the edge of their seats.

— *TAKE OVER AT MIDNIGHT,* LIBRARY
JOURNAL

M L. Buchman's ability to keep the reader right in the middle of the action is amazing.

— LONG AND SHORT REVIEWS

The only thing you'll ask yourself is, "When does the next one come out?"

— *WAIT UNTIL MIDNIGHT,* RT REVIEWS,
4 STARS

The first...of (a) stellar, long-running (military) romantic suspense series.

— *THE NIGHT IS MINE,* BOOKLIST, "THE
20 BEST ROMANTIC SUSPENSE NOVELS:
MODERN MASTERPIECES"

I knew the books would be good, but I didn't realize how good.

— NIGHT STALKERS SERIES, KIRKUS
REVIEWS

Buchman mixes adrenalin-spiking battles and brusque military jargon with a sensitive approach.

13 times "Top Pick of the Month"

Tom Clancy fans open to a strong female lead will clamor for more.

Superb! Miranda is utterly compelling!

Miranda Chase continues to astound and charm.

Escape Rating: A. Five Stars! OMG just start with *Drone* and be prepared for a fantastic binge-read!

The best military thriller I've read in a very long time. Love the female characters.

SIGN UP FOR M. L. BUCHMAN'S NEWSLETTER TODAY

Other works by M. L. Buchman: *(* - also in audio)*

Action-Adventure Thrillers

Dead Chef
One Chef!
Two Chef!

Miranda Chase
Drone*
Thunderbolt*
Condor*
Ghostrider*
Raider*
Chinook*
Havoc*
White Top*
Start the Chase*
Lightning*

Science Fiction / Fantasy

Deities Anonymous
Cookbook from Hell: Reheated
Saviors 101

Single Titles
Monk's Maze
the Me and Elsie Chronicles

Contemporary Romance

Eagle Cove
Return to Eagle Cove
Recipe for Eagle Cove
Longing for Eagle Cove
Keepsake for Eagle Cove

Love Abroad
Heart of the Cotswolds: England
Path of Love: Cinque Terre, Italy

Where Dreams
Where Dreams are Born
Where Dreams Reside
Where Dreams Are of Christmas*
Where Dreams Unfold
Where Dreams Are Written
Where Dreams Continue

Non-Fiction

Strategies for Success
Managing Your Inner Artist/Writer
Estate Planning for Authors*
Character Voice
Narrate and Record Your Own Audiobook*

Short Story Series by M. L. Buchman:

Action-Adventure Thrillers

Dead Chef

Miranda Chase Origin Stories

Romantic Suspense

Antarctic Ice Fliers

US Coast Guard

Contemporary Romance

Eagle Cove

Other

Deities Anonymous (fantasy)

Single Titles

The Emily Beale Universe
(military romantic suspense)

The Night Stalkers
MAIN FLIGHT
The Night Is Mine
I Own the Dawn
Wait Until Dark
Take Over at Midnight
Light Up the Night
Bring On the Dusk
By Break of Day
Target of the Heart
Target Lock on Love
Target of Mine
Target of One's Own
NIGHT STALKERS HOLIDAYS
Daniel's Christmas*
Frank's Independence Day*
Peter's Christmas*
Christmas at Steel Beach
Zachary's Christmas*
Roy's Independence Day*
Damien's Christmas*
Christmas at Peleliu Cove

Henderson's Ranch
Nathan's Big Sky*
Big Sky, Loyal Heart*
Big Sky Dog Whisperer*
Tales of Henderson's Ranch*

Shadow Force: Psi
At the Slightest Sound*
At the Quietest Word*
At the Merest Glance*
At the Clearest Sensation*

White House Protection Force
Off the Leash*
On Your Mark*
In the Weeds*

Firehawks
Pure Heat
Full Blaze
Hot Point*
Flash of Fire*
Wild Fire
SMOKEJUMPERS
Wildfire at Dawn*
Wildfire at Larch Creek*
Wildfire on the Skagit*

Delta Force
Target Engaged*
Heart Strike*
Wild Justice*
Midnight Trust*

Emily Beale Universe Short Story Series
The Night Stalkers
The Night Stalkers Stories
The Night Stalkers CSAR
The Night Stalkers Wedding Stories
The Future Night Stalkers

Delta Force
Th Delta Force Shooters
The Delta Force Warriors

Firehawks
The Firehawks Lookouts
The Firehawks Hotshots
The Firebirds

White House Protection Force
Stories

Future Night Stalkers
Stories (Science Fiction)

ABOUT THIS BOOK

ALICE PAINTS NARROWBOATS THAT CRUISE THE UK CANALS. Her reputation shines as sterling as her art. But when her mentor retires and leaves the company to her, she becomes paralyzed by the task.

Carl simply brought in his parents' boat for a new paintjob. But nothing prepares him for the life changes wrought when he meets the artist.

How can they possibly make two uncertain tomorrows, and hearts, merge like two rivers on the canal?

1

———

"You're *what*?" Alice felt torn in two.

One moment she'd been deeply immersed in painting a very tricky letter S. The owner of this narrowboat had wanted ornate rather than more traditional lettering. *Samson's Strength*, with its four strong S's, was a name he was immensely proud of. It was also a choice that still befuddled her. John Samson was as bald as a cue ball, so his boat's name said he'd already lost his mythical strength. Her attempts to delicately point this out had only led to mutual confusion when he asked who Delilah was and what she had to do with his boat's name. Alice had desisted.

"I'm retiring." Vincent repeated. "It's the first of April, but this is no Fool's Day joke."

Too abruptly, she'd now been rammed into this new moment, making her head spin. It was a change she couldn't reconcile at all with her artistic headspace. She'd been in the flow, her paintbrush soaring with the pinnacles of a Bach organ Cantata through her earbuds.

Bach and Handel were best for lettering work. Mozart and Beethoven were acceptable. After that period, the romantics took over with their over-orchestration and excessive flourishes. They were all *after* the peak of the golden age of canal boating, making them feel too anachronistic when she was working.

"You can't retire." She looked at Vincent, half through her fall of blonde hair and half in the clear. Alice had learned the hard way to never touch her hair while painting, the colors went from hand to hair instantly, no matter how sure she was that her hands were clean. And the one time she used turps, her hair didn't behave or smell right for days.

"Try me. June First, the wife and I are taking that quest I always talked about."

"Boating every mile of the United Kingdom's canals?" He'd talked about it ever since she'd been a little girl, but she'd never thought he'd actually do it. There were over four thousand miles of them. At a canal boat's speed of four miles an hour that would take some time.

"And then we're off to the French canals. After a lifetime of fixing up canal boats, it's time I enjoyed traveling in one."

"But...I don't understand."

His puzzled look had her opening her mouth and then closing it when she couldn't think of how to explain herself. Vincent was more than a mere fixture in her professional life.

She tried again. "I was born here."

He nodded his grey head and smiled. When had Vincent's hair gone grey? She'd never really noticed it before. Sure, she'd incorporated first the shifting grey and later what she thought of as his *distinguished silver* into her color palette but it was still a surprise to fully register it atop his head. They'd celebrated his seventieth birthday only last month.

When Mum had been in her late teens and come off a holiday fling with a narrowboater only to find herself alone and pregnant, Vincent had taken her in. Alice herself had been born in the narrowboat docked alongside Vincent's shop: K&A Lion, Boat Painters. *You just popped out of the rabbit hole, honey, quick as a bunny. That's why I named you Alice. No time to rush off anywhere. No need either. You and me? We did just fine.*

Mum had never had the knack for working on narrowboats. Instead she'd worked for Vincent's wife Edda in the attached K&A Lion, Pub until Alice was grown. Then she'd had a fling with an American on a narrowboat holiday, married, and now had a second family in Austin, Texas.

"Retiring? But who will run K&A Painters?"

Vincent's smile went radiant. "You will!"

Alice wondered what rabbit hole she'd fallen down. It was mid-morning. The sun shone from above. Two boats rested quietly in the shop's painting slips, waiting to be tended to. But nothing was connecting properly. She could only stare at him in disbelief.

"You've always had it in you. You did your first signboard at age eight. By twelve you'd done your first boat stem to stern. Who else would I possibly sell it to?"

"But," Alice waved her paintbrush and nearly splattered the S in *Strength,* which would be very annoying. She'd already had to take it out once because the curves were all wrong. S's were easier to remove entirely and then retry; attempts to fix them as-is never came out right. "But I can't afford to buy a business."

Vincent appeared to be enjoying her complete discomfiture, "You haven't asked me the price."

"I'm not going to." She set her brush down firmly on her palette, a twelve-hole muffin tin caked thick with a hundred dried colors and currently filled with the four active ones. And in doing so, she polluted her brush with a splash of yellow that was for the boat name's *glow of strength* effect, not the lettering itself. She might have to redo the entire name now if she couldn't exactly match the *virile-red* that John Samson had chosen.

"Ten quid."

She eyed Vincent. He was still offering that annoying smile, but he didn't appear to be joking.

"Oh, give over, Alice. Who else would I ever leave it to? Our boy is gone. You're as close as we ever had to a daughter. Edda was always careful with the coin and has sold the pub for a small fortune, far more than we'll ever need to keep us afloat. We don't need the money. Besides, what else would you possibly do? You were meant for this."

2

SHE WAS MEANT FOR THIS?

It had been two weeks since he'd told her, and her throat still constricted too much for her breath to escape.

It had taken Alice four tries to create the final S in *Samson's Strength* and she still wasn't thrilled by it. The owner had been ecstatic, so she'd kept her doubts to herself as he wrote the generous check with a nice tip and motored out onto the Kennet and Avon Canal to show off his fresh-painted narrowboat.

She surveyed the small dockyard that was K&A Lion, Boat Painters. It was her whole world. The double wide shed roof covered two slips for a pair of narrowboats. Seven feet wide and up to seventy long, they had originally carried coal, grain, and passengers from Bristol port and through Bath. From there they'd continued upward along the Avon River, the K&A Canal—where they passed this shop at the top of the Devizes locks, the top of the whole system—and then down the Kennet and Thames Rivers to London at the far end. The same route had carried wealthy Londoners this direction to the social whirl and thermal waters of Bath.

Starting in the mid-1800s, the trains had nearly wiped out the canals. But ambitious volunteers, followed by a great deal of tourism, had brought them back since the 1960s. And Vincent had started K&A Lion, Boat Painters here in Devizes fresh out of secondary school during that resurgence.

The shed roof kept off the rain, the skylights and open sides let in the sun and a gentle wind. The docks were very low to the water to properly paint the freeboard's sides. Redoing the bottom paint in a drydock was left to the repair yards to tackle; K&A was only about the upperworks. Vincent had cobbled together a way to gather the sanding dust so that none drifted onto the other boat, if there were two in the shed, or into the canal waters.

There wasn't an inch of this place that she didn't know—but she'd never wanted to *own* it.

Vincent dealt with the business. With the prices and payments. The schedules. The customers, my word—the customers! All she did was paint the intricate and ever-changing designs on narrowboats.

Nearly all boats bore a large panel on either side, near the stern. Three feet high and six-to-eight long, this was where most of the boat artist's effort typically landed. The boat name, owner, port-of-call, and the builder, if it was known for the more historic vessels.

Some owners desired clean lines and a simple look. Others wanted elaborate re-creations of a luxury that had probably never existed traditionally but were now accepted as such. Complex geometrics, lush flower arrangements, and highly stylized lettering. And yet others broke all *classic* bounds with fantastic or modernist designs.

Her boat, that she and Vincent had slowly fixed up over the years, was tied up along the canal side of the boat shed. Now it served as their best advertisement, easily visible from the canal and adorned with the finest paint job of them all. It bloomed with whimsical flowers, Victorian lettering (she'd listened to a little Chopin while painting those), and all backed by a boat-long glowing sunrise. Mum had named her and the boat on the same day. Not only *Alice's* signboard, but the entire length of the boat abounded with the whimsical characters of *Alice In Wonderland* frolicking among the flowers. The boat depicted the many sights of Wonderland.

Through the years she'd painted everything from block letters to dark wizards creating the signboard name like a flowing incantation.

Her favorites were when the owners dedicated a section of the panel to: *Make something pretty.* She answered with: flowers, castles, prancing horses, woodlands... Woodlands were the best but she loved them all.

It didn't matter to her what they wanted, as long as they were happy. She threw herself into every panel and every boat.

Vincent had trained her and together they'd spent over a decade making K&A Lion, Boat Painters *the* lauded name up and down the canal. It was rare that either slip under the shed roof was empty for more than a day or so and they often had a waiting list.

She stood at the end of the dock, letting the water calm her while she awaited the next arrival. Her favorite duck family clustered nearby with a fresh float of seven downy chicks. Tossing bits of bread, they welcomed her like one of their own.

But *on* her own? Alice had no idea how she was going to go on with her life without Vincent.

3

CARL ALMOST RAMMED THE BOAT SHED AS WELL AS THE... vision standing at the tip of the finger pier. The century-old Bolinder engine designed to move a narrowboat at four miles-per-hour over dead calm water wasn't exactly a powerhouse when it came to emergency reversing of his twenty-five-ton craft.

Thankfully, the vision was as quick with a boat pole as she was lovely.

She'd been standing at the end of the boat painter's dock, her long blonde hair floating about her in soft ripples that caught the morning sunlight. Sparkles of the sunrise skipping low off the main canal, played across her features, turning her from human to fairy princess. Her white painter's pants were more multi-color paint spatters than fabric—she'd been thoroughly Jackson Pollacked. Her maroon t-shirt with a roaring golden lion and the company name outlined her slim figure. The sunny smile she offered definitely reached those brilliant blue eyes despite his clumsy arrival.

She must think him an utter fool. That he ended up tied safely in the slip was far more her doing than his. This had been his family's boat since he was a little boy, and he'd been steering it on summer holidays like an old salt since his teens. But suddenly he was handling it like a pathetic gongoozler.

"Hi, sorry about that. I don't know what came over me."

She offered another shot of that radiant smile. "Any docking made without killing people is a good one."

It was easy to join in her laughter over the old saying as they introduced themselves. He shut down the engine in the cockpit as she snugged off the stern line that he'd handed over.

"You didn't send any drawings or photographs, so let's go over what you want on your boat."

"My parents' boat actually." He hung onto the cabin-roof handrail as he clambered out of the cockpit and edged along where the hull met the cabin.

Narrowboats by their very nature had little spare space above or belowdecks. On top of its sixty-six feet, the rear cockpit had a stand-up tiller and a pair of bench seats that made six a friendly crowd. The distant bow had room for two couples to relax and enjoy the sunset with a post-cruising glass of wine.

The rest was a trunk cabin that ran the length of the boat with a narrow six-inch lip to either side. There was just room for his toes and the balls of his feet as he shuffled sideways hanging onto the roof. At the midpoint, he snagged the spring line that he'd flipped up onto the roof when departing his parents' over-winter mooring a half hour ago.

He hopped down onto the dock, secured the midpoint of the line that was tied both fore and aft to keep the boat steady at the dock, then rose.

He was suddenly mere inches from nose-to-nose contact with Alice.

He was surprised enough to stumble back and land against the boat. It was a good thing he *had* secured the spring line first or he might have fallen into the gap between the boat and the dock.

"Uh, sorry. Being clumsy."

She smiled in a way that said something was amusing her. Perhaps she liked buffoons. Not a role he would normally choose. He was more the confidant center-of-the-business-presentation sort.

"I, uh," he shook his head to clear the slight hypnosis that the lovely painter offered by standing calmly before him. She was exactly what he'd expect if Lewis Carroll's Alice had grown tall and graceful. He turned to the boat.

The *Diana* had generous windows down either side past the rear decorative panels. A tiny container garden of herbs and flowers would sit on the roof all summer. But the paint job was showing its age. The block lettering had merely looked tired until he'd seen the boat *Alice* docked out front, then it had looked—

"Alice!" He turned back to look at the lovely blonde.

"Yes?"

He glanced over the *Diana* toward the boat sitting along the canal. They shared a name. "Is that yours?

Mum always insisted that we slow down to a crawl each time we passed it. She adores the *Alice*. Absolutely stunning." He was fairly sure he was talking about the boat.

"Thank you. Now, your boat?"

Carl cleared his throat but it did nothing to clear his head. "It's their fortieth wedding anniversary. As a surprise gift, I wanted to get her repainted. The whole length, full decorative work, not just a coat of paint and the signboard name."

"With what?"

He could only shrug. He didn't really know. "I, uh, want it to be beautiful."

Again that musical laugh. "An homage to Princess Diana?"

"Uh, no. Mum and Dad are Oxford professors. She's a specialist in Ancient Greek and Roman literature; he's a leading translator of Middle English. That's how we were able to spend summers on the canals each year," he was babbling. "And that's where I learned to handle a boat, which— I need to shut up now after that last demonstration. *Diana,*" he took a deep breath and tried to focus, "is for the Roman goddess, the Huntress."

If he'd thought Alice had been smiling before, he'd grossly underestimated the meaning of the word. She...glowed.

"You're giving me a whole boat to paint—based on a Roman woodland goddess—in any way I want as long as it's beautiful? The goddess of the hunt?"

It sounded a little stupid that way, but he shrugged a yes.

Her squeal of delight would have sent him stumbling back against the boat again if she hadn't hugged him tightly in her joy. It only lasted an instant but it fired off every nerve ending in his body.

Their contact had been electric. At least for him.

Her reaction, however, was to begin frantically mumbling to herself. "Oh my God— Oops!" she bowed to the boat. "Oh my God*dess*. I need my sketch pad. Oh thank you. Thank you. Thank you." She briefly grabbed his arm with a grip most guys at his London gym would envy, then rushed away still talking to herself, "Not Gregorian chants. The medievalists were also of the church, but the wrong church. That would be wrong. I'll have to go with Baroque. No! Opera! *Aida*. *Tosca*. *Cleopatra*. Strong women. Yes. Yes."

Diana was moored in the inner slip, which lay parallel to the canal. Another boat occupied the outer slip, and her boat was tied up beyond that.

Alice raced to the head of the dock, raced over to the outside dock, and practically sprinted to the *Alice* narrowboat, before disappearing below.

Carl stood there, alone on the dock except for a few ducks asking if he had bread, and wondered what had just hit him. A blonde whirlwind...who wasn't returning. He rose up on his toes to peek over the two intervening boats. Through the window, he could see she was already hunched over a table and making rapid movements that were probably on her sketch pad.

He checked his watch. The lunch meeting in London couldn't wait. Though he stretched his slack time to the limit, she showed no signs of returning.

By the time he left the dock to make the two-hour drive back to the city, it was at a run. For the first time ever, he was about to conduct a business meeting in jeans and a t-shirt.

4

THE STATE OF THE *DIANA* WAS HORRID. PRIOR PAINTERS HAD layered new paint on old. In places it was rubbed to a patina shine, worn quickly thin because of not anticipating where hands would grasp and ropes would rub day after day. In others it was peeling due to failure of the lower layers. She eased away a long strip near the after-cabin door—it wasn't even bonded to the layer beneath. Someone should be shot for not properly texturing the old surface with a good sanding before applying the new coats.

It took her most of two weeks to sand the boat back to bare wood. A belt or disc sander was out of the question, though she was tempted several times. The risk of dinging the underlying wood was too great, and it was beautiful wood. Atypically rich-grained, maybe she would leave it bare as the background. After all, Diana's natural habitat was the forest.

Grinding off so many layers with an orbital sander

took forever but it didn't matter, she wanted it to be perfect.

Not only for the boat's owners, but for herself. Half the time was gone until Vincent and Edda...left. It was the only way she could stand to think of it. How could he do this to her? The amount of time she'd already spent stripping off the old paint had used the bulk of the boat's budget. She knew that was wrong, and stubbornly didn't care.

"I've got no business sense. This is going to be a disaster once you leave. Please take it back or sell it to someone else."

Vincent had smiled in that fatherly way of his, patted her shoulder, and turned back to work on the other boat that had come in: a simple roughen, repaint (with a contrasting trimline), and then the signboard.

He'd taken one look at her Huntress sketches and then insisted that he'd do the other boat himself. Over the next several weeks they worked in side-by-side slips. But she rarely saw him, because she rarely looked up from the project of the *Diana*.

Sometimes she'd be sanding along, with the next-finer grit sandpaper, and she'd come upon a bacon butty sandwich wrapped against the dust or a bottle of cold water that he'd left in her way. Alice would wolf it down, an appropriate analogy for Diana the Huntress' boat, and keep going after mumbling a "Thank you" toward Vincent around a full mouth.

When it was done, when not a single joint had one lurking line of the old color, she finally stopped. The silence was deafening after two weeks of work with buzzing of the orbital sander and grind of the rasp. Bare wood at last.

Vincent came up beside her and they stood looking at the bare canvas of the sixty-six-foot-long boat.

"I couldn't have done it as well myself," he whispered softly.

That didn't give her much comfort.

She'd never questioned her skills in painting. It was only in everything else.

5

Carl stared down at his desk trying to figure out what had just happened.

At least it wasn't the Americans, this time. They always had to go in for the kill, it was in their nature. But no, the unanticipated move had come out of Amsterdam.

One moment he'd been leading the acquisition team through the takeover of a very attractive aerospace manufacturer. Within hours of the agreement being finalized and signed, he'd been called into another meeting—during which their entire company had been acquired by the slippery Dutch. The board had negotiated without him, and had only been awaiting the acquisition of the aerospace company before signing.

Now?

He'd been thanked deeply and given a large bonus for the successful acquisition by the old company, then the new one had given him a generous termination package and a swift boot. Fourteen hours ago he'd been on the verge of having everything. And now? At eight p.m. on a lovely May evening, he'd been asked to make sure his office was cleared out before he went home.

Not knowing quite what he was doing, he'd done so: turned in his pass card to security, and driven out of underground parking—a major perk in the heart of London.

Hours later, almost dawn, with little idea of how or even why he'd driven to where he had, he stopped. He recalled the disconnected towns of Brighton, Portsmouth, Stow-on-the-Wold, Winchcombe, and Bath among others. He'd crisscrossed the much of southern England with no real plan or intent except to drive.

Three in the morning. A quiet country lane... Odd place to stop.

Sells Green, he could see the sign in his headlights. The name was familiar, as familiar as an old friend, though he couldn't recall why at the moment.

Why *had* he stopped here?

Looking down at the blinking red light on the dashboard he saw that he wasn't the one who'd stopped —his car had.

Silence.

Out of gas.

He was on a small slope and used it to roll backward and steer onto the verge before pressing the Engine Off button.

Leaving his suit jacket, but picking up the small box that had been the personal items from his desk, he began walking. Up the climbing road, as that was the direction his car had been going.

The country lane climbed above the flat farmland

that stretched off into the darkness to either side. The night was full of stars. The smell of mown hay and fresh-turned soil lay thick upon the darkness. The silence eased London into no more than a passing thought's echo in the dead of night.

He shied away from the thought. *London,* even as a word, did not sit comfortably on his thoughts and the night felt too comfortable to think.

After a lazy curve, he stepped out onto a low brick-sided bridge and knew exactly where he was. Here the road arched over the Kennet & Avon Canal in the middle of the rural hamlet of Sells Green. The main thing it was known for by narrowboaters was a set of municipal-provided trash bins at the canal's edge, and a sign pointing the way to the Three Magpies pub, 281 meters from the canal. That precise *one* was a nice touch.

They'd be closed now. It was okay. He wasn't hungry. Or thirsty. Or tired.

Numb? But he wasn't cold. Shocked? But he hadn't been electrocuted. London? But thankfully the word skidded off his thoughts.

He descended from the bridge down onto the canal-side towpath and turned east. That was toward London, but afoot it was safely too far off to think about. The tall Caen Hill and the Devizes Flight of locks added to the comfortable mental barrier. There was definitely a closer destination...though quite what it was he'd have to take on faith. A strange day, indeed. Yet on careful consideration, he decided it was better not to think beyond that to quite *why* it had been strange.

Once horses had trodden here to pull the canal boats.

A single horse could easily drag a thirty-ton narrowboat filled with fifty tons of cargo for hours along the dirt way. In modern times the path was paved and had become the kingdom of walkers, cyclists, and families who picnicked down its length.

Tonight, it bore the weight of a lone pedestrian—and no ghosts. At least not any unfriendly ones.

Set down among the trees, the water was as silent as the night. Lights shone off to either side from time to time... There was a sliver of a moon... The water a mirror-smooth companion that looked as if he could walk upon it, though he decided he'd stick with the towpath tonight. Wide and well-paved, it was a sufficient guide.

Some unmeasurable time later, he reached the base of the Devizes Flight. It was officially one of the Seven Wonders of the UK Waterways. Its straight climb up the face of Caen Hill included sixteen consecutive locks that lifted and lowered the boats most of the two-hundred-plus-foot difference between the Avon River behind and the Kennet River ahead.

In the starlight, the long line of lock gates climbing the long hill looked as if some giant had spilled his Meccano set onto the grassy slope.

Nestled in the base of the flight, he could see the outlines of sleeping canal boats tied up along the waterway. Their owners perhaps too exhausted from the five-hour descent to brave the last six locks to the Caen Hill Marina below, or had decided to call it a night when they'd seen the great flight ascending ahead of them.

Going through a lock wasn't complicated, but a long flight like this could laborious. It took a fit person on the lock gate and a skilled steerer on the boat functioning in reasonable harmony. Open the lower gate from ashore by pushing against a long heavy lever arm. And once the boat had driven in, close the gate and cross to the head of the lock. There, fill the lock by opening the sluice gate above, finally open the upper gate to allow the boat to depart. Repeat fifteen more times.

He followed the upward slope on the paved towpath.

Most of a mile later, he finally knew where he was heading even if he was too tired to think of why.

When he arrived, he faceplanted into his bunk and fell asleep with the sunrise.

6

_____

ALICE YELPED WHEN THE FACE APPEARED IN THE WINDOW she'd been working on for half the morning. She'd been outlining the window in faux tree-trunk bark.

The face mouthed a *sorry* then disappeared from view. She tugged out a cotton cloth, wiped the paint streak she'd made on the glass, then carefully folded the stain inward before putting it away. The boat swayed slightly as the owner of the face moved about in the cabin and eventually came out on deck. She resettled herself on the small three-legged canvas folding stool on the dock to look at the man standing in the open bow section.

She barely recognized him. It wasn't that she'd given Carl Mason so little thought since he'd given her the job of painting the *Diana,* though she hadn't. It was that he was so transformed.

He'd delivered that boat dressed like any canal boater: jeans, t-shirt, and trainers.

Today he wore very expensive slacks, leather shoes so posh and polished that it was easy to see that they'd had an atypically hard night, and a button-down of unexpected seafoam-green that caused his dark brown eyes to glint like smoked topaz.

She remembered him as handsome.

Now he would look powerful...if he wasn't so wrinkled. The neat wave of dark hair stuck out sideways in a sleep-cowlick. The shirt and slacks had absolutely been slept in.

"What tie do you wear with that gear?" She couldn't help smiling at his rumpled image.

"Uh," he looked down at his chest as if he had no idea what he was wearing, "a colored one?"

She giggled at him. "Try apricot or even a dark coral if you're feeling brave."

Again, that slow self inspection, "I can't say that describes me this morning."

"Go with a sapphire blue then." She turned back to eye the base coat of her faux tree trunk before he could look at her again with that bewildered expression so clear in his dark eyes. "Avoid burgundy unless you want to be mistaken for a Christmas elf."

But even out of the corner of her eye she could see him simply standing there, looking...purposeless. And slightly dazed.

"Oh. I'm sorry. You came to see the progress on your boat." Then she inspected the unpainted length and winced. After that she went out for what Mum called one of her babble-runs. "I'm really sorry that I don't have more to show you. I know it's been weeks, but the old paint job was so awful, and the one under that, and the five or six below them. It's cruel to take wood all the way down like this too often, but it simply needed to be done. I've now laid down a three-layer undercoat that, if treated well, should prevent that being necessary for a long time to come. I did capture a few images of some of the history of the boat as I sanded off layers. They could make an interesting little photo album for your parents. The lowest layer I was able to date was from the 1860s when she was a bawdy-boat."

"A bawdy-boat?"

She could feel her cheeks heat, looking at him fresh from his bed. "*Go for a ride on the canal. Ladies included in the ticket price.* Though maybe they'd rather not know about that piece of its history."

His laugh sounded half normal and half surprised to find itself out wandering along the dock. "No, they'd love it. You want bawdy tales? Read the Greeks, though Chaucer's Wife of Bath would fit in well, too. I can't wait to tell them. You're sure?"

She nodded.

"Isn't that a lark?" He chuckled once more. "But I didn't come to check up on you. It already looks so much better simply being clean."

"Then why did you come in a business suit on a Wednesday morning? You look like the kind of person to be in one of those fancy London high rises."

And his momentary joy collapsed again.

"I...was."

7

AND AGAIN THE CONFUSION RETURNED. CARL WONDERED IF he'd become Alice in Wonderland's hookah-smoking caterpillar, on the edge of transforming, but who the hell knew into what.

He was...here. Talking to the lovely, level-headed painter who was doing something she passionately loved, less than twenty feet from her own floating home that was perhaps the prettiest boat on the whole of the UK canal system.

He too was here, but that was all. His BMW Z4 Roadster was three miles away below the Devizes flight of locks, out of gas on a back country lane. Two hundred kilometers from the nearest change of clothes in his high-rise mid-town condo. And about a kilometer more from the office that filled his life—*had* filled.

No! He'd brought more with him. Of more importance, though he had no idea what. He'd carried a box of the essentials from the car last night and they were here, on the table downstairs. He wondered what the hell he'd found so important from his old life to hand-carry from the car in the middle of the night when he didn't even know where he'd been.

His old life? How could that be his *old* life? His old job, sure. But he wasn't here to change his life.

Alice had returned to her painting. How long had he been standing like a zombified...zombie?

"I'm headed below. I'll try not to rock the boat."

The briefest slide of her hair was the only indication that she'd heard him. She was lost in her world in a way he'd never been lost in his. He was good at it, and he'd liked how that skill made him feel. Earned him a lot of nice pats on the back, then he remembered the bonus and severance package, and a lot of money. But she was absorbed wholly by the art of creating, he glanced down —a tree trunk where there'd never been a tree trunk.

He soft-footed his way below and went to inspect what he'd thought was so precious that he couldn't leave it locked in the car's trunk.

First, Carl scrounged up an old packet of tea from last summer's cruising and a tin of biscuits that Mum always kept handy in case of a breakdown far from a town with a market. Was that it, was he having a breakdown? Because he could think he'd had one, did that mean he was already over it? He checked his watch. Under twelve hours ago. Not really enough to call more than a *lapse*. He'd had a couple of college benders that had lasted longer.

Once his tea was steeping, he dunked a stale biscuit into it and munched as he sat at the table. His family had shared thirty summers of meals here. Mostly good times.

Any bouts of sullen teendom had been abandoned ashore at the start of each summer.

Carl opened the small box. It was no bigger than three reams of paper and it was all higgledy-piggledy rather than tightly packed. A little from this drawer or that, rather than gathered by any conscious plan.

A picture of the three of them hamming it up in the cockpit when he was in his teens. He could always start Mum and Dad going with a mangled quote from disparate sources. *Romeo and Juliet* recast with the characters from *Oedipus Rex*. The Old English monster Grendel recast as Juliet's nurse had been one of his favorites. He wished he'd recorded some of the improv plays that they'd spontaneously fabricated together, but they were all lost to happy evenings along the canals. They never happened at home, where the quiet harmony of ancient studies would squeeze down until he'd thought his head about to explode before it would ever break free into the modern world.

Still, below the photo lay his copy of Chaucer's *Canterbury Tales*, in the original Middle English of course, and the eleven surviving plays of Aristophanes *not* in Greek, because he could barely struggle through that. A stack of pads of lined-yellow paper, and a long thin box.

He knew what was inside. He'd always kept it in his top left desk drawer, of college and each job, though he had rarely opened it over the years.

This time he did and looked down at the shining black and gold Waterman pen.

A fine mind needs a fine pen, Mum had said. And Dad had added, *Water Man? You get? Si? Si?* In the voice of

Manuel from *Fawlty Towers*. They'd given it to him on their last night together on the narrowboat before he'd left for college.

They understood nothing of what he did in the modern business world as it didn't impinge on their own interests buried not centuries but millennia in the past.

His view of the pen had shifted over the years. At first fascinated by it, he had attempted to recreate the family farces, though he rarely made it past a page or so. For a while, he'd used it to write witty mash notes on fine parchment with a neat hand that had occasionally earned him laughs—and more often than not had turned into lovely epistemological adventures. Now, if it didn't have a direct plug-in to cloud or display up-to-the-minute business news analyses, it wasn't worth consideration.

Except it was one of the few objects he'd taken with him last night.

Why this out of everything?

8

ONCE ALICE BEGAN PAINTING A BOAT, IT WAS PRIMARILY AN intuitive process. The forest built quickly. At first only the occasional fox, squirrel, or owl could be glimpsed wandering through.

But then a delicate white horse-like animal, just now wandering out of sight behind a window, showed a shining horn reaching past the far side of the opening.

Two days later, Alice was sure that she spotted a baby griffin preening on a high branch, so she filled it in. The next day, a pair of tiny dragons were roasting marshmallows over each other's flames.

The creatures were often shadowed, barely discernable. But if a person took the time, the forest was populated with everything from dormice to pegasi—though Carl had absently informed her that the proper plural was pegasuses.

With no explanation, he had moved onto the boat.

First, he had departed with a can of gas, then been back a few hours later with a metallic-blue sports car, that he'd called a Misano blue. It wasn't really any proper blue but rather a wandering baby chick lost somewhere in the land not occupied by azure, cobalt, or lapis. Simply because they could make a new color didn't mean they should—it was attention-grabbing, but had no proper emotion attached to it once it had forced her to look its way.

Early the next week, he'd been gone for two days, with hardly a word.

He'd returned with a brand-new two-door Mini Cooper Electric in proper British Racing Green. It was so cute, she wanted to hug it.

It had been stuffed to the gills with boxes, which he was kind enough to leave stacked at the edge of the dock until she was done for the day. When she'd offered a hand loading them aboard, he accepted happily.

"Haven't slept much in a while, so I'll take all the help I can get," as they handed boxes first from dock to boat and then from on deck to down below.

"Why not?" She peeked around the inside of the boat. It was like a slightly rumpled living room, well lived in and comfortable. The interior woodwork had fared far better than the exterior, it looked cherished rather than abandoned.

"Well, let's see." He cracked open a box and began unloading books onto the breakfast nook table. She was bemused by the fact that they were mostly cookbooks. "Seven days ago I had a serious bankroll job, a car that was all about my ego, and a Thames-side apartment meant to make women weep with joy." Then he grimaced. "Uh, sorry about that."

Like she hadn't already known that someone as handsome as Carl had women flocking to him. "Did it work?"

Again the grimace. "Yeah, I guess. At first anyway."

"What happened then?" To keep her hands busy, she quickly sorted the cookbooks by region, then thought better of it and resorted them by color and began to shelve them close by the kitchen.

"I stopped taking time off from the job. Not a lot happens with women when you never take time off."

"Ah," she didn't comment on her own similar tactics, *keep busy; keep men at bay.* The way men looked at her made their preferences obvious. She'd made enough early mistakes to wait for the quiet and kind ones rather than the handsome men-about-town. Though none had reacted with quite the shocked expression, or the attempt to destroy his narrowboat when he'd first seen her, quite the way Carl had.

"Yep, I bought all the way in. Got a wake-up call the evening before I landed here."

"Seven days ag—"

"Nope!" He cut her off as he dug open the next box and began shifting clothes into a small set of drawers. "Seven anything is too short a timespan for me to be making this kind of change."

"Geological epochs?" she teased him.

"Nope, still way too short," he really smiled at her for the first time since his arrival last week. "How long is one of those anyway?"

She shrugged. Alice actually had no idea either.

"Doesn't matter. So, my life's story of the last seven

whatever-really-long-time things?" He broke down the boxes and handed her two bags before waving her toward the kitchen.

She glared at him.

He caught the full blast—and laughed. Her glares were supposed to be more effective than that. "No, sorry."

He was still chuckling and she was considering hitting him with the smaller bag, which was rather heavy with tin cans.

"I meant for you to stow them on the galley shelves, not cook for me. God, it's been so long since I took the time to cook a meal for myself. I miss it." He nodded toward the cookbooks, cocked his head for a moment at her rainbow-spectrum organization, then nodded again as if that worked for him.

She felt silly for overreacting. "I can barely boil noodles." She'd grown up eating in the pub kitchen each night with Vincent, Edda, and her Mum.

"It always seemed that my parents could live on poetry, as long as it predated the dinosaurs. I learned to cook on this boat as a matter of survival. I'm glad to make us dinner in thanks for your help when we're done here." And he carried another load of belongings down the narrow aisle to the master bedroom.

She began stowing things randomly in the cupboards as his voice drifted to her down the long cabin. What did she know about how to organize a galley? Almost as little as she knew about running a business.

"Seven of those long-time-things ago, I had a job and career that made perfect sense. Six LTTs ago, after driving my car until it entered a fume-free state over in

Sells Green, I walked here. For five days, I sat here watching a beautiful woman do something she was completely passionate about. Which left me to wonder what I was passionate about."

"You said you enjoyed your job." They had actually talked very little over those days. Except for sharing quiet sunsets sitting alongside the canal, Carl had rarely left that table in the center cabin except for meals in the pub.

"Right," they met back at the shrinking pile of boxes. "Enjoyed because I was good at it. Not because the job itself was much fun or did anything to inspire me. It made me lots of money and offered only fleeting joy. I bet you aren't like that."

She could only shake her head. "Me? I love thinking of every boat I've ever painted, sailing somewhere along the canals and making their owners happy. It's like I'm spreading cheer over the land. Of course, it doesn't make me wealthy enough to live in a fancy London apartment like yours."

"Would you want to if it did?"

"You're joking, right?" He didn't look like he was though. "Uh, no. I like the size of my life." And she was once again reminded *that* was going to change in two more weeks, one way or another. Vincent insisted they were going. Edda had tried talking to her as well, but something inside Alice knotted past tolerance each time the subject came up until she could neither speak nor hear.

The unchanging arc of her life since birth was about to be broken. Whether or not she took over the business, her life would never be the same.

"Yeah, it doesn't fit me anymore either. That's why I traded in the car and sold the apartment. That's where I was over the last two days. This is now the size of my life." He patted the stack of boxes and looked around the boat. "The only thing I don't have is clear knowledge whether I'm being brilliantly insightful or having a mental breakdown."

9

―――――――

ALICE TOO WONDERED THAT, ABOUT HERSELF, AS SHE discovered a red squirrel family perched in an ash tree on the aft quarter of the *Diana*.

Unlike his first days on the boat, when he'd rarely spoken, Carl had become relaxed and voluble. The two faces of drama: tragedy and comedy. He'd received one but decided to consciously make it into the other.

When she'd asked over dinner what he was planning to do, he had shrugged. *No need to rush, between the job and condo sale I'm set for quite a while. Years. Maybe,* and he'd laughed in surprise, *decades if this becomes the scale of my lifestyle.*

And while he'd spoken, he'd toyed with a small metal case that rested on the edge of the table.

10

———————

THEY SPENT ANOTHER WEEK PRACTICALLY COHABITATING ON the boat. *Practically* because he slept inside at night and she worked on the outside during the day. He was often gone from breakfast to dinner, always afoot with a small pack. The little green Mini never moved from its parking spot. Snooping through the boat's window, she saw that the small box was never there on the table during the day.

In the mornings they'd share coffee, a pastry, maybe a few words as the day started quietly. She appreciated that, as she was typically organizing her night's thinking into what would become the day's painting.

Dinner, however, was a different affair. He made sumptuous meals or organized a gourmet picnic that they would take to the head of the Devizes Flight of locks to watch the narrowboats make the traverse. He'd been trained by two classicists and she'd learned history through art. For hours they would sit and discuss topics that ranged across Europe from the

Socrates to Banksy. Half the time it was reality and half more fanciful than even the creatures on the *Diana* or the *Alice*.

The first time she'd kissed him had been along the Devizes Flight up the Caen Hill. He'd been creating a fairy tale made of King Arthur's knights calling up the ghost of Socrates to help them determine a battle plan, but the old man kept insisting that it was time to discuss shadows created by the flickering fire.

When Carl had revealed that Socrates had actually been taking whispered instruction from a dormouse napping on his shoulder, she'd been unable to help herself. She'd kissed him.

The first time she'd slept with him, it had been in her bed aboard the *Alice*, which he'd been surprised to find had been painted very simply as a cozy burrow that a badger or hedgehog or even a Hobbit—if it wouldn't be in the wrong story—might enjoy.

It wasn't that he was the best lover she'd ever had, though he was. Rather, Carl's bravery at forging a new path, whatever it might be, had lit something inside her that she didn't recognize. But she rather liked it.

"I've never been a deep thinker," she informed him one night when she woke to find the moonlight dancing through her bedroom windows.

"Nor I in my past."

"But you are now?"

Carl considered a while with his head upon her breast. "I'm not sure. I have a theory."

"Filled with fabulous creatures and peculiar non sequiturs?"

His light laugh rippled from his jaw to her breastbone. "I don't think so but I can try if you'd like."

"I *love* your stories." And she did. Whether he was telling tales of fancy, of history, or of some event in his life, his voice, his *words* carried her there. To that place that built so richly in her imagination.

"Uh, thanks," he said it a little stiffly, but before she could ask why he hurried on. "There's only one kind of stupid, but lately I've been thinking that there are many kinds of smart."

"I barely made it through secondary, except for my art classes." She wanted to be more than merely pretty. She could feel his London Business School masters even if he never hinted at the vast chasm that it created between them.

"That's irrelevant. You are utterly brilliant."

All she could do was scoff at him. "You just like being in my bed."

"I do, but that's not my point. Seriously, Alice," she could feel Carl's smile in the night. "And how many times did Alice tell herself to be serious in Wonderland of all places. Anway, you have this amazing painting ability."

"That's a skill, not an intelligence."

"No argument, but you didn't let me finish. You apply that skill with an emotional intelligence and a sensitivity that makes you loved up and down the length of the canal. I ran into your bald-headed captain of *Samson's Strength* one day when I was walking along the canal. And despite a complete lack of understanding of Biblical mythos, he couldn't offer enough praise when I mentioned you were doing my parents' boat. Yet it looks nothing like mine, which looks nothing like yours. In fact, I've been trying to spot your work as I walk past the boats and the only common factor I've found is that they utterly stand out. Each person I ask, confirms that it is your work and how much they love it. I have no idea how you do that, but it's utterly brilliant."

She kept her thoughts to herself on those points. Unlike most men, Carl never made her feel stupid or uneducated or ignorant. But brilliant? Not by any measure she understood. Time for a subject change.

"What color is your intelligence then?"

"I thought it was business. I understand the shape and nature of how businesses fit together. But the more I think about all those years, the more I think that falls into the skills category."

And that's when she heard the fear in his voice. He wasn't blithely dumping one lifestyle and tumbling into another. He was seeking more, more of himself. That was the moment Alice knew she had embarked on no simple fling. Her lover was afraid, which only made him all the more brave. She didn't know what his *intelligence* was— beyond convincing her that she was wonderful in more ways than she'd ever imagined—but she knew he possessed more of it than any man she'd ever been with.

She slid her arms around him and held him close. Held him until he fell asleep, leaving neither of them convinced.

But as she stroked his hair and watched the moonlight shifting through the tall trees bordering the canal, perhaps they were both hopeful.

11

"Alice," Vincent's voice landed somewhere between pleading and annoyance and he interrupted her work on the outer side of the bow.

She tried to find last night's hope, but despite whatever intelligence that Carl was so convinced she possessed, she wasn't very good at finding it.

"One week. Edda is ready, the boat is ready. When we hand over the pub, we hand over our flat above as well. The business is yours whether you want it or not. If you decide to close it, that will be up to you."

She neither wanted it nor knew what she would do without it. She certainly didn't want to be the one responsible for shuttering Vincent's life's work.

"I put no boats on the schedule, but there's already a waiting list as long as the summer. You could keep three of you busy if you wanted to hire some assistants."

That meant employees, which meant payrolls and taxes and more supplies and—

Alice bit down hard on the panic.

She'd be done with the *Diana* by the end of this week as well. What then? Would Carl float away and be gone? Who would fill the empty mooring that Vincent and Edda left behind?

"I'm sorry, Vincent. I shouldn't have delayed you. But I don't know what I'm doing and—" her voice was climbing toward hysteria, so she bit it off hard.

Against his normal practice of disappearing during the day, Carl had come back. He was standing at the head of the dock looking quizzically at the two of them standing by the *Diana's* bow.

"Um, should I come back later?"

Alice could only look down at her knees and shake her head miserably. Vincent had given her two months' warning and for all her vaunted *intelligence,* she'd taken no action.

"Is everything okay?"

She shook her head again.

12

————

AND THAT, CARL KNEW, WAS HIS CUE. THOUGH HE HAD NO idea of his first line now that he'd made his grand entrance. That would teach him to forget his slicker when it was raining out.

He sat on the gunnel of the *Diana* and faced Alice perched on her little painter's stool. Vincent, who he'd shared a beer with as they'd both watched Alice work late yesterday evening, stood—at a loss—a few steps away. By some silent pact, he hadn't asked a single question about Alice or how she was related to the old man. Instead, Vincent had used a style not so different from one of Mum's gentle inquisitions. It had Carl spilling much of his past, though none of his current doubts.

"You two at odds feels very wrong. Can I help?"

Alice's head remained down and Vincent scowled at him. Well, this was a good start—if he wanted Dante's Virgil to lead him on a ramble through hell.

"I've known her since three months after she was conceived, what would you know that could possibly help?" Vincent snapped. Skip the ramble, Carl was being dragged straight into the ninth circle.

"I know nothing about what's going on so maybe I can lend an impartial ear." Only the rain pattering on the shed roof's skylights answered him.

Vincent grunted then dropped back to sit on the fresh-painted boat in the other slip.

"No!" But his call was too late and Vincent's butt hit wet paint.

He shoved to his feet leaving an additional palm print on the fresh paint to match the stripe on his bum.

"That'll teach this old man. Beginner's mistake." He fished a cotton cleanup rag from Alice's stack and used a splash of turps to clean his hand.

"I'll fix it," Alice mumbled miserably. "It's all my fault that—"

"Hell you will, Alice. I painted this boat. I sat my old bum down on it, so I'll fix it. But not until we fix this." He flapped a sheaf of papers at her that he'd tucked under his arm while cleaning his hand.

"May I?" Carl held out a hand.

Vincent glared at him before practically slapping them in Carl's face as he handed them over. "Okay, Mr. Businessman, you go ahead and find a single goddamn thing wrong with those." Then he stalked away down the dock muttering to himself about having to remix the paint colors.

Carl had analyzed five-hundred-page contracts covering massive mergers and acquisitions. This was a half page transference to Alice of all rights belonging to

K&A Lion, Boat Painters. Its property, assets, client list, bank accounts, and appointment book. For—

"Ten pounds?"

Alice still hadn't spoken.

"And you aren't leaping at this because...?" In a past life, he'd have finished that with *you're stupid.*

"Because I'm stupid," she finished it for him. "Go ahead and say it, I heard the thought."

"I didn't say it because you aren't."

"But that's what you're thinking, right?"

He flashed back to last night's discussion in her arms about not being a deep thinker. He hadn't been. His education, business acumen, women, his *life* had always come to him easily, so why waste time thinking about it. These last weeks he'd done more deep thinking than the whole of his life combined.

"No-oo. Not the new me, anyway. The old me might have, but the more time I think about him, the more I'm convinced he was an idiot and I'm better shut of him."

For the first time, she raised her gaze enough to glance briefly at him with those piercing blue eyes. "There's only one me. This one," she waved at the *Diana,* which wasn't going to be just the envy of the canal, it was going to be the envy of an art museum. "Not that one," she waved at the papers in his hand.

He looked at the other pages. Legal deed to the property. Most recent balance statement that showed a nicely profitable business of long standing. And a multi-page long waiting list of boat name, brief job description, and contact information. The final page was a schedule sheet for the two slips...and it was blank. Vincent had scheduled nothing ahead, awaiting Alice's decision.

"Is there some catch here I don't understand? Does Vincent have some hold over you or—"

"He's the best man who ever lived!" And there was a fire in her eyes that was completely new to him.

"Should I be jealous?" Carl did his best to make it a joke. "Not sure I like the idea of someone other than me holding that much of your heart."

It seemed to work. Alice reached out a hand and brushed his cheek. "Mum landed here as a pregnant nineteen-year-old. Vincent and Edda took us in. Raised me like I was one of his own. His son died in Afghanistan by the time I was ten. Vincent gave me..." she shrugged "...everything."

"And now he's trying to give you the business."

"Yes."

"And?"

"The *business.* I'm a business idiot. All I've ever done or known to do was paint boats. Do you think it makes one instant of sense that I've spent six weeks exclusively on your boat? Budget?" She splayed her fingertips off her temple hard enough to foof a brief wave through her hair. "I blew that four weeks ago and didn't care."

"I'll pay the difference."

She shrugged. "I'm not asking for—"

"I'll pay the difference. I already guessed that and told Vincent. It's worth it to have the boat done right for my parents."

"Oh. But that's not the point. Vincent is leaving. He always ran the business."

Carl stared down at the papers. He could run this operation on twenty minutes a day. Schedule, money, budget, and stay out of the painters' way. Add a couple staff and it could be seriously profitable.

But it wasn't his place.

If this relationship ended, he'd be gone and she'd be stuck with a disaster of his making. He couldn't do that to her. Nor did he like the sound of the *ending* part of that thought.

He had never so enjoyed being with a woman. Every moment he was with her, new vistas of possibility opened up for him. Would he have walked away from London if he hadn't had the vision of Alice living along the K&A Canal that was so filled with happy memories of his own? Probably not. He'd certainly received enough calls from headhunters to join any number of prestigious firms. In the last week, New York, Tokyo, and Singapore had all called.

These few precious weeks had been an awakening in every clichéd sense of the word. He'd spent long mornings walking along the canal and long afternoons writing ideas with that pen Mum had given him. He'd have to switch over to a computer soon, but the framework for a novel—a fun, fantasy romp filled with goddesses and humans—had somehow passed through the filter of falling down the *Alice's* Lewis Carroll-type rabbit hole was all there. He was rediscovering his youthful joy of writing something other than business proposals.

That too was easy to lay at Alice's feet.

"You inspire me," the words slipped out in a whisper to dance upon the morning light.

"I what?"

He focused more clearly upon her. "You. You're the one I want to tell my stories to. You're the one who keeps opening doors I didn't know existed. These last weeks I've been...happy! Happy without knowing I was sad before. Except I wasn't sad. So I suppose you've made me happ*ier*. Please tell me how to make you happier."

13

___

Happier? Had she ever been *unhappier*?

Alice had never in her life argued with Vincent before. He was father, mentor, and confidante-best friend all rolled into one. When her snarky teen hormones had her and Mum in a stand-off, Vincent was the one she'd turned to.

"I'm hurting him. I know I'm hurting him. And it's killing me." She couldn't keep the anguish out of her voice. She'd never been able to. Her emotions always shot straight to the surface before she even knew they were there.

Carl took her hand, then brushed at the tears she hadn't known were there.

He waited, but she couldn't think of any words to say, even if she could speak. All she could do was hold onto his hand and wonder if he could keep her from drowning in her own inadequacy. Wouldn't Lewis Carroll have the last laugh if she did—a real lake of tears.

"Okay, I could make a stupid offer, but I'm not going

to. I could step in as a business partner and run it for you, but we're at the beginning of us. I really like this beginning, but I know that's all it is. It's good enough that I can't wait for the next step, but we aren't there. So that isn't the answer."

She really liked their beginning too. No one had ever made her feel so appreciated for herself. But he was right, it wasn't the answer. And that made her feel that much closer to Carl that he saw that—rather than trying to *rescue the poor little bird*. Still, it wasn't enough.

Carl flipped through the sheaf of papers then laughed a little to himself. "Let's try twenty questions."

She had a thousand. What she didn't have was any answers.

"First, is there anything in the world you'd rather be doing than painting boats? Fine art? Dance? Modeling, which you certainly have the looks for? Nuclear scientist?"

The last elicited a laugh that was only partly choking sob. "Anything in the world? How would I know? I've never been anywhere except along the canals. Mum and I joined Vincent and Edda on holidays, but they were always boating holidays."

"Nowhere exotic? Not even down the rabbit hole?"

She smiled toward her own boat. "Not outside my thoughts. You?"

"A lot of places...for work. Mostly I saw loads of near-identical conference rooms. Not much of anywhere else for me either."

Alice began studying Carl's fingers because she could feel him studying her face and doing some of that deep thinking of his. They were good hands. Not callused, but strong. She liked the way they felt in hers. She liked the way she felt in his arms. And she'd miss him when—

She gasped. She never thought ahead about anything. "What?"

"When I finish your boat, where do you go? Does all this end?" It felt as if her heart had been painted over with a hard acrylic.

"My parents' moorage is about half a mile away."

"And you're staying on the boat?"

"Until I think of something better. They're aboard three months a year, but I have my own room even then."

Again she found a watery laugh, just a little louder than the passing of a narrowboat out on the canal. "See? I don't think ahead. I never thought about you leaving when I finished your boat. Does that sound like a businesswoman?"

"Business isn't your *intelligence*. I could set up some simple steps for you to manage it. Vincent's been doing it so long, I doubt if it's even conscious for him, but I could teach you."

"But if it doesn't work then..." she sighed, "Then I'm right back where I started."

14

And Carl burst out laughing.

Alice could not imagine how what she'd said was in any way funny.

"Sorry, okay. I think I have an answer. Care to take a trip down the rabbit hole with me?"

"I...suppose."

"Good. Do you have ten pounds on you?"

She fished a note out of her pocket and handed it over.

"Sign there," he handed her Vincent's papers. Then he reached into his pocket and pulled out the small metal case. Inside was a lovely fountain pen. An artist's, no, a *writer's* fountain pen. It had his name scribed on it and M&D. "Mum and Dad," he explained.

She was halfway to signing it when she caught herself, "No! Wait!"

He placed his hand lightly on the back of hers and guided it toward the signature line. "Trust me."

And for some reason, she signed.

He took everything back and shook her hand. "Congratulations."

"What have you done to me? This doesn't feel like a rabbit hole, it feels like a bottomless pit."

"All the best rabbit holes do," he smiled. "You now legally own K&A Lion, Boat Painters."

"But—" He stopped her with a finger upon her lips.

"Now comes the rabbit hole part. Ready? Let's go traveling."

"What?" He wasn't making any sense.

Carl smiled. "Let's jump in together. Narrowboat through Scotland, ride motorcycles across the Australian Outback, go to a small Italian cliff town to hike the hills and eat a different flavor of gelato every day for a month. Let's do something, together. Let's find out if we can sail along the same channel."

She liked the sound of that. A lot. She had spent very little money on herself and Vincent had always paid her a good wage.

"And then, whenever you want, you can come back here. Sell the business and start something new. Hire a partner who *does* know the business side. Turn it into your own private studio. Whatever you want. There's good equity here. That means you now have some money and the property is all paid for. Vincent will have done what he wants to most, he'll have set you up as well as he could before retiring. What you do from there is up to you."

Alice didn't know where to look. But she could see

many surprising things she'd never noticed before. Over the last five years Vincent had re-roofed the boat shed, had all of the rotten timbers in the docks replaced, even upgraded what little office equipment and paint storage they needed. He'd done his best to fix it up...for her.

And she *did* love it here. If her life could be spent painting the unending variety of narrowboats, it would be a life she enjoyed.

She also saw a flash of a boy and girl racing along these same docks she had as a child, a place where she'd found so much happiness and contentment.

The man. The one who even now sat waiting for her. It was easy to see him here too. Writing his tales. Novels, plays, magazine stories. It wouldn't matter, because she knew that Carl would find the joy in anything he did.

She watched him as he stood and moved to meet Vincent halfway along the dock. He handed over the papers, the ten-pound note, and shook Vincent's hand. Vincent looked as if he was going to cry with happiness.

Yes, she *would* jump down the rabbit hole with Carl. They would...go see the art of Paris and Florence.

But then she would come home.

Here.

And paint her joy.

But first, there was a Phoenix peeking over Diana's shoulder, near to bursting with the desire to come to life.

———

If you enjoyed this story

please consider leaving a review.
They really help.

Keep reading for an exciting excerpt from:
Where Dreams #1: *Where Dreams are Born*

WHERE DREAMS ARE BORN (EXCERPT)

IF YOU ENJOYED THAT, YOU'LL LOVE THIS TALE!

WHERE DREAMS ARE BORN
(EXCERPT)

RUSSELL LEANED HIS BACK AGAINST THE STUDIO DOOR after he locked it behind the last of the staff. He barely managed the energy to turn off his camera.

He knew it was good. The images were there; he'd really captured them.

But something was missing.

The groove ran so clean when he slid into it. First his Manhattan high-ceilinged loft would fade into the background, then the strobe lights, reflector umbrellas, and green-screen backdrops all became texture and tone.

Image, camera, and man then became one and nothing else mattered—a single flow of light, beginning before time was counted, and ending its journey in the printed image. One ray of primordial light traveling forever to glisten off the BMW roadster still parked in one corner of the rough-planked wood floor worn smooth by generations of use. Another ray lost in the dark blackness of the finest leather bucket seats. A hundred more picking out the supermodel's perfect hand dangling a single shining and golden key—the image shot just slow enough that the key blurred as it spun, but the logo remained clear.

He couldn't quite put his finger on it...

It would be another great ad by Russell Morgan, Inc. The client would be knocked dead—the ad leaving all others standing still as it roared down the passing lane. This one might get him another Clio, or even a second Mobius.

But...

There wasn't usually a "but."

And there definitely wasn't supposed to be one.

The groove had definitely been there, but he hadn't been in it.

That was the problem. It had slid along, sweeping his staff into their own orchestrated perfection, but he'd remained untouched. That ideal, seamless flow hadn't included him at all.

"Be honest, boyo, that session sucked," he told the empty studio. Everything had come together so perfectly for yet another ad for yet another high-end glossy. *Man, the Magazine* would launch spectacularly in a few weeks, a high-profile mid-December launch, and it would include a never before seen twelve-page spread by the great Russell Morgan. The rag would probably never pay off the lavish launch party of hope, ice sculptures, and chilled magnums of champagne before disappearing like a thousand before it.

"Morose much?"

The studio kept its thoughts to itself—the first reliable sign that he wasn't totally losing his shit.

He stowed the last camera with the others piled by his computer. At the breaker box he shut off the umbrellas, spots, scoops, and washes. The studio shifted from a stark landscape in hard-edged relief to a nest of curious shadows and rounded forms. The tang of hot metal and deodorant were the only lasting result of the day's efforts.

"Get your shit together, Russell." His reflection in the darkened window, stories above the streetlights of West 10th, was unimpressed and proved it was wise enough to not answer back. There was never a "down" after a shoot; there was always an "up."

Not tonight.

He'd kept everyone late—even though it was Thanksgiving eve—hoping for that smooth slide of image-camera-man. It was only when he saw the power of the images he captured that he knew he wasn't a part of the chain anymore and decided he'd paid enough triple-time expenses.

The next to last two-page spread would be the killer —shot with the door open against a background as black as the sports car's finish, the model's single perfect leg wrapped in thigh-high red-leather boots all that was visible in the driver's seat. The sensual juxtaposition of woman and sleek machine served as an irresistible focus. It was an ad designed to wrap every person with even a hint of a Y-chromosome around its little finger. And those with only X-chromosomes would simply want to be her. He'd shot a perfect combo of sex for the guys and power for the women.

Even the final one-page image, a close-up of driver's seat from exactly the same angle, revealing not the model but instead a single rose of precisely the same hue as the leather boot, hadn't moved him despite its perfection.

Without him noticing, Russell had become no more than the observer, merely a technician behind the camera. Now that he faced it, months, maybe even a year had passed since he'd been yanked all the way into the light-image-camera-man slipstream. Tonight was a wakeup call and he didn't like it one bit. Wakeup calls happened to others, not him. But tonight he could no longer ignore it, he hadn't even trailed along in the churned-up wake.

"You're just a creative cog in the advertising machine." Ouch! That one stung, but it didn't turn aside the relentless steamroller of his thoughts speeding down some empty, godforsaken autobahn.

His career was roaring ahead, his business' growth running fast and smooth. But, now that he considered it, he really didn't give a damn.

His life looked perfect, but—"Don't think it!"—his autobahn mind finished despite the command, *it wasn't*.

Russell left his silent reflection to its own thoughts and went through the back door that led to his apartment —closing it tightly on the perfect BMW, the perfect rose, and somewhere, lost among a hundred other props from dozens of other shoots, the long pair of perfect red-leather Chanel boots that had been wrapped around the most expensive legs in Manhattan. He didn't care if he never walked back through that door again. He'd been doing his art by rote; how god-awful sad was that?

And just to rub salt in the wound, he shot *commercial* art.

He'd never had the patience to do art for art's sake. Delayed gratification was his idea of no fun at all. He left the apartment dark with only the city's soft glow through the blind-covered windows revealing the vaguest outlines of the framed art on the wall. Even that almost overwhelmed him tonight.

He didn't want to see the huge prints by the *art* artists: autographed Goldsworthy, Liebowitz, and Joseph Francis' photomosaics for the moderns. A hundred and fifty rare, even one-of-a-kind prints adorned his walls—all the way back through Bourke-White to Russell's prize, an original Daguerre. The Museum of Modern Art kept begging to borrow his collection for a show...and at the moment he was half tempted to dump the whole lot in their Dumpster if they didn't want it.

Crossing the one-room loft apartment—as spacious as the studio—he bypassed the circle of avant-garde chairs that were almost as uncomfortable as they looked and avoided the lush black-leather wrap-around sectional sofa of such ludicrous scale that it could be a playpen for two or host a party for twenty. He cracked the fridge in the stainless-steel-and-black corner kitchen searching for something other than his usual beer.

A bottle of Krug.

Maybe he was just being grouchy after a long day's work.

Juice.

No. He'd run his enthusiasm into the ground but good.

Milk even.

Would he miss the camera if he never picked it up again?

No reaction.

Nothing.

Not even an itch in his palm.

That was an emptiness he did not want to face. Especially not alone, in his apartment, in the middle of the world's most vibrant city.

Russell turned away, and just as the door swung closed, the last sliver of light—the relentless chilly blue-white of the refrigerator bulb—shone across his bed. A quick grab snagged the edge of the door and left the narrow beam illuminating a long pale form on his black-silk bedspread.

The Chanel boots weren't in the studio after all. They were still wrapped around those three thousand dollar-an-hour legs: the only clothing on a perfect body. Five foot-eleven of intensely toned female anatomy right down to an exquisitely stair-mastered behind. Her long, white-blonde hair lay as a perfect Godiva over her tanned breasts—except for their too exact symmetry, even the closest inspection didn't reveal the work done there. She lay with one leg raised just ever so slightly to hide what was meant to be revealed later.

Melanie.

By the steady rise and fall of her flat stomach, he knew she'd fallen asleep while waiting for him to finish in the studio.

How long had they been an item? Two months? Three?

She'd made him feel alive...at least when he was

actually with her. Melanie was the super-model in his bed or on his arm at yet another SoHo gallery opening. Together they journeyed to sharp parties and trendy three-star restaurants where she dazzled and wooed yet another gathering of New York's finest with her ever so soft, so sensual, and so studied French accent. Together they were wired into the heart of the in-crowd.

But that wasn't him, was it? It didn't sound like the Russell he once knew.

Perhaps "they" were about how *he* looked on *her* arm?

Did she know tomorrow was the annual Thanksgiving ordeal at his parents? The grand holiday gathering that he'd rather die than attend? Any number of eligible woman would be floating about his parents' house out in Greenwich; anyone able to finagle an invitation would attend in hopes of snaring one of *People Magazine's* "100 Most Eligible." They all wanted to land the heir to a billion or some such; though he was wealthy enough on his own, by his own sweat, to draw anyone's attention. He ranked number twenty-four on the list this year—up from forty-seven the year before despite Tom Cruise being available yet again.

But not Melanie. He knew that it wasn't the money that drew her. Yes, she wanted him. But even more, she wanted the life that came with him—wrapped in the man-package. She wanted The Life. The one that *People Magazine* readers dreamed about between glossy pages.

His fingertips were growing cold where they held the refrigerator door cracked open.

If he woke her there'd be amazing sex. Or a great party to go to. Or...

Did he want "Or"? What more did he want from her?

Sex. Companionship. An energy, a vivacity, a thirst he feared that he lacked. Yes.

But where was that smooth synchronicity hiding, like the light-image-camera-man of photography that he'd lost? Where lurked that perfect flow from one person to another? Did she feel it? Could he ever feel it? Did it even exist?

"More?" he whispered into the darkness to test the sound. He knew all about wanting more.

The refrigerator door slid shut—escaping from his numbed fingers—which plunged the apartment back into darkness, taking Melanie along with it.

His breath echoed in the vast darkness. Proof that he was alive if nothing more.

It was time to close the studio—time to be done with Russell Incorporated.

Then what?

Maybe Angelo would know what to do. He always claimed that he did. Maybe this time Russell would actually listen to his almost-brother, though he knew from the experience of being himself for the last thirty years that was unlikely.

Seattle.

Damn! He'd have to go to bloody Seattle to find his best friend. There was a possible upside to such a trip— maybe there'd be a flight out before tomorrow's mess at his parents'. He slapped his pocket, but once again he'd set his phone down in some unknown corner of the studio and it would take forever to find. He really needed two—one chained down so that he could always find it to call the other.

Russell considered the darkness. He could guarantee that Seattle wouldn't be a big hit with Melanie.

Now if he only knew whether that was a good thing or bad.

———

Keep reading now!
A great tale of romance and adventure,
Of sailboats, food, fashion, and fun.
Available at fine retailers everywhere.
Where Dreams are Born

And please don't forget that review for Solo Passage.

ABOUT THE AUTHOR

USA Today and Amazon #1 Bestseller M. L. "Matt" Buchman has 70+ action-adventure thriller and military romance novels, 100 short stories, and lotsa audiobooks. PW says: "Tom Clancy fans open to a strong female lead will clamor for more." Booklist declared: "3X Top 10 of the Year." A project manager with a geophysics degree, he's designed and built houses, flown and jumped out of planes, solo-sailed a 50' sailboat, and bicycled solo around the world...and he quilts. More at: www. mlbuchman.com.

Other works by M. L. Buchman: *(* - also in audio)*

Action-Adventure Thrillers

Dead Chef
One Chef!
Two Chef!

Miranda Chase
Drone*
Thunderbolt*
Condor*
Ghostrider*
Raider*
Chinook*
Havoc*
White Top*
Start the Chase*
Lightning*

Science Fiction / Fantasy

Deities Anonymous
Cookbook from Hell: Reheated
Saviors 101

Single Titles
Monk's Maze
the Me and Elsie Chronicles

Contemporary Romance

Eagle Cove
Return to Eagle Cove
Recipe for Eagle Cove
Longing for Eagle Cove
Keepsake for Eagle Cove

Love Abroad
Heart of the Cotswolds: England
Path of Love: Cinque Terre, Italy

Where Dreams
Where Dreams are Born
Where Dreams Reside
Where Dreams Are of Christmas*
Where Dreams Unfold
Where Dreams Are Written
Where Dreams Continue

Non-Fiction

Strategies for Success
Managing Your Inner Artist/Writer
Estate Planning for Authors*
Character Voice
Narrate and Record Your Own
Audiobook*

Short Story Series by M. L. Buchman:

Action-Adventure Thrillers

Dead Chef

Miranda Chase Origin Stories

Romantic Suspense

Antarctic Ice Fliers

US Coast Guard

Contemporary Romance

Eagle Cove

Other

Deities Anonymous (fantasy)

Single Titles

The Emily Beale Universe
(military romantic suspense)

The Night Stalkers
MAIN FLIGHT
The Night Is Mine
I Own the Dawn
Wait Until Dark
Take Over at Midnight
Light Up the Night
Bring On the Dusk
By Break of Day
Target of the Heart
Target Lock on Love
Target of Mine
Target of One's Own
NIGHT STALKERS HOLIDAYS
Daniel's Christmas*
Frank's Independence Day*
Peter's Christmas*
Christmas at Steel Beach
Zachary's Christmas*
Roy's Independence Day*
Damien's Christmas*
Christmas at Peleliu Cove

Henderson's Ranch
Nathan's Big Sky*
Big Sky, Loyal Heart*
Big Sky Dog Whisperer*
Tales of Henderson's Ranch*

Shadow Force: Psi
At the Slightest Sound*
At the Quietest Word*
At the Merest Glance*
At the Clearest Sensation*

White House Protection Force
Off the Leash*
On Your Mark*
In the Weeds*

Firehawks
Pure Heat
Full Blaze
Hot Point*
Flash of Fire*
Wild Fire
SMOKEJUMPERS
Wildfire at Dawn*
Wildfire at Larch Creek*
Wildfire on the Skagit*

Delta Force
Target Engaged*
Heart Strike*
Wild Justice*
Midnight Trust*

Emily Beale Universe Short Story Series
The Night Stalkers
The Night Stalkers Stories
The Night Stalkers CSAR
The Night Stalkers Wedding Stories
The Future Night Stalkers

Delta Force
Th Delta Force Shooters
The Delta Force Warriors

Firehawks
The Firehawks Lookouts
The Firehawks Hotshots
The Firebirds

White House Protection Force
Stories

Future Night Stalkers
Stories (Science Fiction)

SIGN UP FOR M. L. BUCHMAN'S NEWSLETTER TODAY

and receive:
Release News
Free Short Stories
a Free Book

Get your free book today. Do it now.
free-book.mlbuchman.com